Antidote Illusions
A TRISTAN GRIEVES FRAGMENT

ERIK HOFSTATTER

Copyright (C) 2022 Erik Hofstatter

Layout design and Copyright (C) 2022 by Next Chapter

Published 2022 by Next Chapter

Edited by Chelsey Heller

Cover art by CoverMint

Mass Market Paperback Edition

This book is a work of fiction. Names, characters, places, and incidents are the product of the author's imagination or are used fictitiously. Any resemblance to actual events, locales, or persons, living or dead, is purely coincidental.

All rights reserved. No part of this book may be reproduced or transmitted in any form or by any means, electronic or mechanical, including photocopying, recording, or by any information storage and retrieval system, without the author's permission.

I knelt in what used to be her. The blood. It fled out of her wound-torn land. In almost visa-free rhythm. Then angel embryo fell on death's brake pedal. Her essence became a slow tourist. She walked on a blue tightrope—my vein. I heard ichor songs play backwards. A seductive requiem to erotic despair. All inside the moribund strip club that was her body. Or maybe she just gave what was due back to the earth.

Grasshoppers, little grasses. They chirped "murder" somewhere outside. I brushed away red-hair eclipse, blocking the white sun of her face—feeling like king astronomer. Those big, calamity-colored eyes. A gateway to cy(psy)clones. She was a sanity taker. I negotiated with thin shavings from my heart.

"Why them peepers?" Boomerang said, Zippo-scorching his fag. He blew out smoke rings. A nicotine party for a ghost exit. I turned my head, looking at her, but curving words his way.

"They spoke for her spirit sometimes."

"She was a polyamorous mess. Didn't like guys much but dug that genderless soul-accent of yours."

"I'm not a guy. I'm a demi-god." I said, imagining his goblin-grin painted on my back.

"In this neighborhood, why not. You ever got your picture stuck in dead retinas?"

That mood crushing cunt. I collar-grabbed his meaning. Brain slammed it. The last sight myth. Not me. Never me. I was the square-faced polaroid (p) imp/printed on a mascara lane to cocaine heaven.

"Don't tongue fence me."

Wrong night. I felt weak. Piñata sluts assembled on condom littered hemi-fields. All I had for mental defense. His question choice hit hard. Doubt owned me. Miss Paranoia loved me. Was he in there? Face naked, floating eternally, in a round pool, her tears, warm still—what was the temperature of emotional turmoil? My cogitation took a knock.

"Oi. Eye-snatching prince. The night ain't young no more."

I got up and shrugged away higher calling. They did not belong to me. The screen-slave eyes. Only to the tricksters. The L sisterhood. The flint-hearted she-hounds and their 24/7 hunt for adoration. Deep-seated, needing, feeding, on a compliment-built throne. Digital flattery.

The currency into her knickers, where she kept all her secrets. Ego riches collected in an iPhone bank. But how do you patent hyena lust on a love beggar's thinking plate?

"Put her in the ground, man. Let the worms take 'em."

The ferryman on watered time—always moving oars through rough months. My watch reflection showed half-past human. It was a good night to uncork memories, to let them breathe, to taste that '94 sweet-red. I missed her shine. That unhinged mind. How she brought me down with a smile arrow. Straight to my knees like Achilles. Then the phone rang/BoomeRANG.

"Yeah?"

"I need you in Shoreditch."

"To do what?" I said.

"Damaged goods. I want you to sniff out the problem."

"When?"

"How fast does whore cry travel?"

"From fist to fist? I don't know."

The bastard hung up. He pushed me so high on the pimp ladder I got vertigo. Bi-girls rubbed my lamp for summons. I never took E. I took toxic love in a red capsule. You know healthy is boring, right? Bad blood left unclean. The spice between us = unconditional flavour. I thought about quicksilver, sitting on that table, reading my emotional striptease. I drank green fairy advice from a French bottle. She explored my old man anatomy when nights were young. Thoughts re-shuffled to the problem solver I became. I'd leave tomorrow.

The monkey on Kamil's back uncaged the situation. He was an ex-serotonin chaser. The cubed habit buyer. That's what they said. I parked around the corner and silenced the engine. Tranny outcomes came to life in my well-oiled brain machine. Behind those walls they manufactured scenarios. Special of the day: external fried lies. Fat appetite seekers. Our clientele. I hammer-fisted the door.

A hammerhead shark circled. Bloodthirsty Olga. Forehead like a Chernobyl road. Eyes too far apart. She was perfectly imperfect. Do you remember?

"Sup, TG."

I pushed past her attitude. "Kamil gave you that racoon make-up, yeah?"

Her right eye bore pirate flag colours soaked in Vodka tears. The house smelled like stolen passports. Daddy playground manifested. I thought about objectives and re-aligning wrongs. She poured herself more antidote illusions.

"Want some?"

"I'll just drink your aura." I said.

Her skinny arms, un-tanned by the vegan sun. Face like a misshapen danger sign for lust-starved men. Cheap shark rides beneath adrenaline pale. A one-way ticket to cum ocean—her home. She wore many smiles and I undressed them all. That's why Boomerang threw me here. I was the higher mind enforcer, the consequence deliverer.

"Where is he?"

Olga nail-tapped her glass, Morse coding thoughts. The dynamic altered slightly. Her light visage changed to dark guilt. She put quarter-truths to bed. They hid under her warm blanket tongue. Peeking.

"I'll rip your fucking tongue out in a minute. Shake words out of it if I have to."

"There's a problem."

I read torn horoscopes in her eyes. We were star-lings without wings. The unbranched on a tree of life. She pointed at a door where my next headache laid. Maybe I'd borrow her painkiller lips later.

"You gotta fix it, TG."

Her accent was cut from Ukrainian glass—clean and sharp. She gave words a different anatomy. I followed those giraffe legs (my map) inside a private audition room. I thought about girls that came here. All fathered by poor choices. How they kneeled and slurped on erect hope. Their tragedies told through intense dick sucking—you could hear them.

"He's right there." Olga said, hand-gesturing downwards.

The wall spoke second. IN PIMP BLOOD, SHE REMEMBERS HATE. A six-word death sentence sealed in red ink thieved from his criminal veins. Kamil's life-empty body came to view. His face down, drunk and stupid, like it wanted to organize a coup against its own tyrant emotions. I thought of a naked flesh horizon where knives could sail into. Then I thought about her. Liene. The ship that passed in the night.

"I didn't kill him."

"It don't take Rolls-Royce mind to figure that out." I said.

"What do you mean?"

She looked at me, alibi in a lie—parachute ready to lip jump. Dumb bitch. I'd had more luck feeding idiom scraps to the three-legged dog outside the bin.

"Come here. I want to fuck you in front of a dead audience."

~

Bite marks on a scream-washed pillow as I thrusted love into her. The enigma peeler. She dirtied ears and minds with provocative cries. I watched nipples rise from pain sea internalized. When busy hips sank down inches—beneath her face—a secret lust for grinches. My (bomb) shell goddess shone orgasm bright.

"I crown you, King Bareback." Olga laughed.

Those bravado-blue eyes. I lit a smoke and scrolled for Boomerang digits. I was a spokesman for inarticulate massacres. The dark crowd navigator. His voice came after five rings. Musashi deadly.

"What the fuck is going on up there?"

"Someone made Kamil...redundant." I said.

Olga took a drag and her tobacco breath found me again. I felt druid peace inside. She kissed nonchalantly, but magnet strong. I tasted nicotine and my favourite mistake. That addictive smell of sexual dualism—her perfume. You know what I mean?

"Good. I never liked the prick."

"He got pricked for blood in the end."

"Funny," Boomerang said, "you just got promoted. Congrats."

"There's more."

"More what?" he said.

"Writing on the wall. In pimp blood, she remembers hate. I heard that phrase before."

"From me, yeah. So?"

"So how did it get there? And why?"

"What exactly are you asking me here, Tristan?"

I herded selectively bred thoughts for unethical slaughter. Olga shark-toothed my shoulder. We watched sugar cube funeral on Van Gogh absinthe spoon. It burned down heretic fast.

"She in the ground?"

"Permanently, brother. She's worm food. Now sort this shit out and call me when it's done."

Olga mixed our drinks and sank into a corner—legs open for Vincent's sugared face. She pressed it against her clit. Her moans transmitted loud on pleasure frequency 201.

A liar's fury gets tattooed on you. In octopus ink. Her escape mechanism. It ate thought paths ahead. Fragments of her ran backwards and down. Away from me. Into that space beyond the sun. Olga—the nocturnal cash hunter—was gone. I brushed my teeth with alcohol and unboxed the charade in my head. Boomerang AKA seller of faked words and gold-plated promises on a foreign whore market.

And Liene. The dust that never settled. I

pulled her again from my mind archive. *In pimp blood, she remembers hate*. That hate restaurant had a blood reservation in my name. Her every breath shortened mine. Trust but verify. Maybe she was in the ground. Or maybe her revenge pulse was loud enough to push away dirt and mud. A she-golem built from old betrayals. I got up to a systematic door knock.

"Yeah?"

Katerina walked in. A sparkly dark ruby dress, tight around her body. Like she was wrapped in curtains of Moulin Rouge. She pushed a cup of coffee in my direction. Black. The surface of a Monday mood. Her hand shook when skin brushed skin. I stood in dry eye corners where sorrows used to rain.

"Thanks. I heard you got moved here after what happened."

"Business is a lot faster here, man. Brothel El Dorado."

"Drop the unfazed act."

"What?" she said.

"Death bit my family too. You can't put a muzzle on that bitch."

The heart remembered hard truth acrobats. Her blinking spelled out denial. I bottled the glue that held her fractured reality together. She got high on it. We sat on the bed stained with unachieved orgasms.

"I don't know what you mean."

I drank more coffee from slut kitchen. Katerina was a hedgehog in a cage. Jutting out words I had to turn and twist and pull to free the captive meaning. Sometimes it took hours.

"The death of your sister. I get the scenery change."

"Sister?"

I casted eyes on that blank canvas. Emotions carefully painted in identical white. That vulnerable camouflage. Hard to see. But it was there.

"I don't have a sister."

"Not anymore you don't." I said, dragging nicotine down throat alley.

"No, I never had one."

The room became a calculator. It divided us. 4 x 4 thoughts. They multiplied in quiet numbers. I breathed out many false sums. Then I deducted bullshit and arrived at her mother. The grief facilitator. A century beak in a feather temple. Feeding on soul grains. What if, right?

"How's the mother of all erasers?" I said.

"Who?"

Her thorn fortified mind cuts your questions —just to watch uncertainty bleed. She gave no plasters. That forced me to change tact. Find a looser tongue. Somewhere. On the coast lit by her aura fire. Maybe.

"Don't worry. What you want?"

"Olga's downstairs with Kamil's body. She needs your help."

~

My portrait hung in the Devil's gallery. He sketched it years ago. People always remembered looks from below/a sin glow—burned into far memory. I envied peace on dumb faces. Cruising through one-way thoughts. They begged no one for the mind gag, when all I wanted was to flee out of my head and get love asylum in yours. But you turned my soul anorexic. You starved me out.

"A little help here?" Olga said with that sea killer accent. I watched her roll up the carpet. Kamil resembled a human cigarette smoked by Hades. The downward God that fucked him. In a moment framed in green I said: "Get him outta there."

"What?"

"I'm jealous."

"Of?"

"His flatline heart."

We swapped places and she sushi wrapped me. Cosmo-quiet. I felt like a present with a suicidal name tag. A dead gift to your vanity, found inside the maze you put me in. *You, ever the pain stalker*. I slept in a carpet once before, for warmth, squatting in a flat south of Brno. But you? You were the winter no clothes could prepare me for.

"You're fucked up, TG."

Her words lived in dead air when I thought about you. How it felt to be your love martyr. How you sponged my heart with afterlife soap. Now I was a carpeted half-corpse. A spinning viewpoint of a hell-gate pointer. The cruelty appointer. Portions of you, too small for my bite.

"What do you know of Katerina's mother?" I said.

Olga slouched. Uncertainty heavy on her. A little headshake.

"Not much. Kat said that her mother lived in the trees. She was drunk."

"In the trees where?"

"Baker Woods. Why?"

"Bird watch. Now move. We'll toast his ass downstairs."

Do you miss my love drops on your tongue? The rearview mirror reflected eyes where crow feet prints got stuck. You know the past hurt eyes—where strayed birds mudded your heart. Shame I owned them. External journey upshots done lengths in a square glass pool. But the real

VIP soul scars exhibition was underneath. *If you're not going to swim deep with me, then get out of my waters.* I gave you gills and you gave me chills.

I exited my modern chariot, feeling thin. Had nothing but oxygen sandwich. Orphaned leaves skipped around me. Some drowned in the puddles. I dodged branches wind soldiers bent to their will. She came from the Baker tree. I pissed harsh words on her sometimes to help her grow. But I was just another totem pole you carved with your lie symbols. The woods held a green umbrella over my head.

Ant kingdom hustlers sold warning signs. I was never a caution taker/only a reckless eye-contact maker. Music notes swung from tree to tree to me. A paradise melody. Chords taught in angel schools. This had to be your mother.

"You remember her songs?" said a joyful voice in Eden accent.

Her songs. I spent my life in them. Inside raw truths and organic hearts. No traces of chemical delusions sprayed by your brain pesticides. Just soft sung words unscrewing tears. Spat on emotions cleaned in ultrasonic voice. That's what you sounded like.

"My name is Tristan."

"I know who you are, Sirin."

"And who would that be?"

"The bringer of death. And death you brought."

The bird juggled seven positions up in the tree. I had no names for all those wing colours. Gold licked them. And crimson. Burgundy, maybe turquoise. Then she dropped down to a crooked branch. Her talons dug deep. Wood heroes screamed. She parted wings to show me skin that could outrun the sun. I knew she caught many eyes in that breast trap. But I was weak. My mouth gaped open—a stadium where I hoped her nipples would come to perform. Then I saw her face and felt cactus desire. Parched.

"You're thirsty," she said and flew straight down to our common ground. She wore body jewellery in sheikh's weight. And a head harness that ruled many stones. Her hair—the colour of angry Etna. Somewhere between 800 and 1000 Celsius. Her temperament felt much hotter.

"And you're hungry."

My jacket pocket carried a prime cut finger parcel. She liked the dead pimp sauce. I fed her all ten. Guess Kamil got to finger her in his own way. But I was the one ruffling feathers. Always.

"Why did you come back here, Sirin?"

"Katerina. She can't remember her sister. Thought you might."

"She wished to forget grief, yes, to bury emotional pain."

Don't ever bury your lessons. You paid for them with aches. When you lift heavy emotions day to day—strength grows. Your brain gets hench. That was always your flex. Like nothing could hurt you. But I could. The weight of my eyes, crashing into you. One rep and I got you weak.

"It's true then. Liene is dead." I said.

The Alkonost charm corrupted thought flow. She rose to rainbow height. Her wings swept life dirt away. Sharing space with her, in a ring of immortal energy, made me feel new. Recharged to 100. The bird woman came close and found my ear.

"You enjoy tempting fools. When they're stupid enough to buy tickets to your egomania."

"What do you mean?"

"You know exactly what I mean. You became a world flier, staying in human hearts like hostels. Your mind is a polyamorous trophy shelf. You're nothing but a bipolar gaslighting champion with a dual sexuality and an empty soul."

"You don't know me."

"Oh but I do, Sirin. I know the artwork your fans leave behind."

"What artwork?" I said.

"Their corpses. Lives lost to the heart thief. I

hoped in time—my love would cure you of that pathological narcissism. That I alone would chase out the chase you had to feel."

"You're delusional. I only came to ask about Katerina."

My tone got heated. Maybe from the by-standing sun. It turned around and moved in with trouble clouds. Like it no longer wanted to listen. What do you do when even the sun don't want you?

"Katerina loved you. She'd follow you anywhere."

"And Liene?" I said.

She resurrected something in me. That undead tomb monster I can't escape. I remember you there. *I want everything in this place, including you.* But feelings mutate. Every day. Not mine.

"Liene hated you for the attention you seeked from anyone who wasn't us. She hated your ghostship logic and how it steered you away into that selfish mist. She wanted revenge."

"You can't kill a death bringer."

Dark trees took her then. I stood alone again with living pillars. Solemn wood faces told me to go. I got clarity in pure answer mash I ate from her mouth. Bird to bird. Liene was really gone. But someone wanted me dead. Brothel wall words. IN PIMP BLOOD, SHE REMEMBERS HATE.

"I got a job for you." Boomerang said, palms pressed together in Buddha prayer. Rolex Explorer climbed up his once poor wrist. Now he was a status flasher. Lady Ambition rode shotgun in four rings built for him in Germany. He parked her outside ivory tower realm for Trojan types that infect. A HQ for short skirt commandos crouching on dick terrain every night.

Cum shooters needed constant target practice. I shot you in the mouth too. *Bang bang*. Four white bullets you took for me. My DNA soldiers died on your big tongue battlefield. I—

"Are you listening?"

More shots. A whiskey glass boomeranged to me. It wasn't coming back. I held it close. It glowed like amber kryptonite against the light of my mood. Something he gave to veterans fighting in the cunt wars. I drank and nodded.

"Good. You got a new girl coming in tomorrow. I want you to show her the ropes."

"I ain't no dick pleaser, man. Olga is."

Double round hit our bloodstream again. I felt organs heating up. Even the worms you left on my heart began to sweat. The room got dark. It ate few shades off your perfume bottle.

"You're the labia merchant. And this one's got a special pussy vintage. 18 years old."

That dropped a foot on my thought pedal. I always won a trophy in the gash race. But I'll never forget crashing my helmet into you.

"And I'll get a taste, yeah?"

Boomerang lowered his head, jackal sly. "Maybe. I opened her mind so let her breathe for now. Let her circulate around the house. She'll acclimatize soon enough."

"If I can't fuck her, what's the point?" I said, knocking back burning hell. The alcohol walked through seven veins, down and down, like Dante.

"She's lost. You know that bin bag identity. You set shit up for yourself, then you find ways to self-sabotage, conjure the right excuses, anything to convince yourself that it's okay to just throw it all away cos you don't know if it's really *you*."

"I know the type."

"We all do, brother. Sad existence. You drift through life, not knowing who you are, you see pieces of yourself in other people, so you covet, walk in their shadow, wanting what they want."

"And that's the paradox. You blame high-fliers for knowing what you don't."

"Exactly. You cut a key shaped like your complaints and you lock yourself away in a jealous cell of your own making. And you hide there. Well. I want *you* to help her break out."

"I'm not a psychiatrist, man."

"No, but you're a limit breaker."

"The only limit I want to break, is my whiskey intake." I said, splashing insides with his booze. My 'damaged goods' roll ran out with you. You were taped head to toe with it. You walked through the door, all dressed in warning signs. High voltage. You sat down and you plugged yourself into my eye sockets. I felt you instantly.

"She's upstairs. Just take her under your wing."

"My wing is broken. What exactly you want me to do?"

Boomerang dropped eyes back to his Explorer. A model that climbed mountains. Not him. His hands only climbed the silicone kind. "We'll get her working soon. Help her settle in the new nest."

One more drink. A quick whiskey vitamin for the sorrow demons. Make their teeth strong for the bite fest later. I finished what Boomerang couldn't. The bottle in my hand was empty glass. Old legs carried me to someone new. Each step a small country. I've seen Lisbon, Paris, the east coast of Canada, even the Caribbean—but nothing could beat that African sunset. I wrote telepathic letters sent to you through 1st mind class. You read them when moon was your bed lamp.

"Are you Tristan?"

With the height of the stairs came flesh scenery. She looked sub-tropically hot. Tall. A model for straightjackets. Prozac suited her. Eyes threw good instinct daggers. I thought of her skin—moisturized with future cum. Then I spun a finger in a pirouette signal. The girl spoke my ballet language. She turned and jiggled her moneymaker in a well-practiced rhythm. Right against my crotch. I got dick tremors and gave her 20 for the warm-up. Saw my other fantasies printed on that note. She sweated porn star confidence. Always a + in this business.

"Very good. What's your name, darlin'?"

"Reyna."

I imagined her up there, pushing clouds together. Rubbing out rain babies. Then dropping them on you. I thought of your naked body housing orphaned gifts from her sky. She smelled like unapologetic cruelty. Maybe that's where she got her rain. Tears on tap. You pulled on me and my barrel never ran dry.

"Wanna fuck me?" she said.

Thoughts gathered to her pussy reyn. And me. The labia cloud separator. Rubbing screams out of you. I earned you that night, when you moaned the name of kings.

"Let whiskey fuck us first." I said, sauntering to the Italian globe bar. That Da Vinci rust. Wooden countries X marked by your lipstick. New lands. More love slaves for your pharaoh charisma. You kissed in hieroglyphics. I poured 2 glasses. Isle of Skye. Half an island in each. Salut.

"Who was she?"

"What?"

"I can almost see her pasty legs, dangling from your frown." Reyna said. She flipped 180 again and rode her dress up and parked above waist. Calvin Klein lady boxers. They ate her ass cheek where the Devil put a little pimple. My dick got Medusa stone hard. I grabbed her hips.

"She was nobody. Just an avalanche. Came at you hard. And cold. Sometimes."

"You like cold seasons? Where I come from it's always warm..." she said, guiding my hand down along a smooth thigh. A slow lane for a Ferrari pulse. But something felt unfamiliar. I pushed her away and shock crashed.

ABOUT THE AUTHOR

Erik Hofstatter is a dark fiction writer, born in the wild lands of the Czech Republic. He roamed Europe before subsequently settling on English shores, studying creative writing at the London School of Journalism. He now dwells in Kent, where he can be encountered consuming copious amounts of mead and tyrannizing local peasantry. His work appeared in various magazines and podcasts around the world such as Morpheus Tales, Crystal Lake Publishing, The Literary Hatchet, Sanitarium Magazine, Wicked Library, Manor House Show, and The Black Room Manuscripts Volume IV. Other works include Rare Breeds, The Crabian Heart, Punishment by Hope, and the Tristan Grieves fragments, beginning with Soaking in Strange Hours.

To learn more about Erik Hofstatter and discover more Next Chapter authors, visit our website at www.nextchapter.pub.

Antidote Illusions
ISBN: 978-4-82415-579-5
Mass Market

Published by
Next Chapter
2-5-6 SANNO
SANNO BRIDGE
143-0023 Ota-Ku, Tokyo
+818035793528

7th November 2022

www.ingramcontent.com/pod-product-compliance
Lightning Source LLC
LaVergne TN
LVHW032014070526
838202LV00059B/6457